☆ CHAPTER ONE ☆

"Who wants to audition for the school play?"
The booming voice of Mrs Ironglove echoed
through the school assembly hall. "Come on,
don't be shy, this is your chance to be stars..."

Owl's heart thumped so loudly that it
threatened to drown even the Ironglove's bellow.
She longed and longed to act, but did she dare to
try? Owl gazed in awe at the towering figure of
the Ironglove, with her steely hair, steely eyes and
sinewy arms. Her shimmering grey suit looked as
if it were fashioned of chain mail. Mrs Ironglove
was the drama teacher – and she certainly knew,

thought Owl, the meaning of the word 'drama'.
She left a meaningful pause while her eyes swept
the rows of pupils like a steel
broom, before once more
booming out.

"Come on, come on,
I'll read out the list
of characters and anyone
who wants to can put
their hand up for each one.
Now... first, elves. Who
wants to be an elf?"

Owl thought that just
possibly she dared to be an
elf, but she was frozen to the
spot, surrounded by a
forest of eager waving
hands. Why was everyone
else so keen? And why did
none of them seem to be shy at all?

Mrs Ironglove scribbled the names of
volunteers furiously as she swept through the cast

list. Now she didn't pause at all: everything seemed to happen so fast that she had already covered trolls, sprites, squirrels, toadstools, vulcans, goblins, soldiers and handmaidens – while Owl was still frozen with fright.

"It's now or never," thought Owl desperately and, terrified, gulping for breath, with a superhuman effort, she shot up her hand.

A ripple of laughter surrounded her. "Oh no," thought Owl, "what have I done?" She realised with a chill of terror that she had just volunteered to audition for the lead part – a part that was totally unsuitable for her...

"No laughing," snorted the Ironglove "we're all equal here, even..." her voice trailed off as her eyes fell on Owl and she realised that the shyest girl in the school (and by far the smallest in her class) had just put her hand up.

"You had plenty of time to go to the toilet before we started, you'll have to wait," said the Ironglove looking severely at Owl. Everyone giggled.

"She's just been, Miss," said a lanky girl about three times Owl's size.

Mrs Ironglove peered harder over her spectacles. It had never occurred to her that Owl might want to audition. This was little Emily Smith, the girl who looked like a baby owl and who would never speak in class assemblies. She wouldn't even admit it was her birthday, in case she became the centre of unwanted attention.

"Are you sure you want to go for that part, Emily?" she asked quite kindly.

Owl was speechless with fright.

"Well, why not?" smiled Mrs Ironglove, seeing the tiny girl's embarrassment. She thought to herself that little Emily had a lot of courage. "Auditions start next Wednesday," she continued. "Copies of the play on my desk. Only for those wishing to take part," she hissed, as several pupils surged forward to nab the play.

Owl joined the queue to get a copy of the play.

"What are you thinking of being?" murmured the tallest boy in her class in Owl's ear. "Is there a part in the play for a hamster?"

"Maybe you could play some of the scenery, instead," added his friend.

"The only thing she could play is pass the parcel," hooted another. The teasing went on and on. Not for the first time, Owl wished she were at the same school as the rest of the Fab Four. Surely this wouldn't happen if her best friends were there to support her? Or at least she wouldn't feel so bad.

After school, Owl trailed home dejectedly and raced up to her room to hide the play from her family. She could just imagine what her big sister Loretta would say if she knew... Sure enough, she had hardly thought the thought when Loretta came bouncing into her room (without knocking, of course). Owl shoved the play under her pillow and sprawled on the tiny bunk bed in an attempt to look casual. Luckily, Loretta didn't notice her strange pose.

"Guess what kid? I got the leading part."

For a moment, Owl couldn't think what she meant. How had Loretta, who had left school, got the lead in her school play? Then she realised. It was her big sister's dance class that she was talking about.

"W-wow, L-Loretta, th-that's just great." Owl reluctantly hugged her sister. Loretta would be a star. Loretta had always known she would be a star. That was the kind of confident person Loretta was. And Owl had to sadly admit that she deserved it. She was bright, articulate, talented, a

brilliant dancer and tall and beautiful, and, thought Owl sadly, all the things that Owl wasn't. As Loretta glided out of the room, Owl plunged her face into her pillow. What a fool and an idiot and a no-good dumbo she was. Too shy to speak up for herself when it really mattered and yet now, somehow, she had been crazy enough to volunteer for something that would just make her feel even more stupid and hopeless. Not just the lead part, but what a part! It was hard to imagine anything more unsuitable for Owl...

Her miserable reverie was interrupted by the phone.

"It's for yoo-hoo," warbled Loretta.

Owl hurriedly wiped her face dry on her sodden pillow and stumped downstairs. It was probably Mrs Ironglove, ringing her at home to advise her against the audition. How humiliating!

"Y-yes?" she mumbled.

"Owl! It's me!"

"Oh, Eclaire," muttered Owl. Normally she would have been thrilled to hear from one of the Fab Four, but at this moment she could hardly raise a smile.

"Oh great. You sound really pleased to hear me," Eclaire said, in her usual bouncy way. "Never mind, I'm trying to get a Fab Four meeting together, for tomorrow at my place. Can you come?"

"Why? What's happened," asked Owl suspiciously.

"Nothing. That's just the problem. We're all fine, but we're all bored. I want to make something happen. Can you come?"

"I d-don't really feel like it," said Owl, in a distinctly trembly voice.

"Oh come on Owl, we can't meet without you."

"I th-think you can easily m-meet without me," said Owl, in her gloomiest whisper. "I can't do anything, anyway."

"Owl, what on earth is up? Of course you must come. You're not doing anything else are you? Come on, spill the ketchup," Eclaire was suddenly suspicious. Maybe Owl had something more important to do.

"N-no," Owl immediately wished she had thought of an excuse, but she never could seem to tell lies.

"Well then, you'll have to come. Obviously there's something wrong. You can come and tell us all about it. Then the meeting will have a real point. See you at my place at 5.30. OK?"

"Er... OK. Bye." Owl put the phone down and tramped back upstairs. She couldn't bear to go to a meeting, she couldn't bear to admit her stupid mistake. Miserably, she felt under her pillow for the dreaded play. She leafed through it. The leading part was vast. She didn't have the heart to read it. She would just have to tell Mrs Ironglove it had been a mistake, that she had just put her hand up to go to the loo after all...

☆ CHAPTER TWO ☆

Owl spent all the next day at school avoiding anyone who might have seen her put her hand up for the audition. She glimpsed Mrs Ironglove at lunchtime but didn't have the courage to approach her. As the day dragged on, she realised that she wanted to go to the Fab Four meeting. She wanted to pour her heart out to them. They would understand, surely... wouldn't they?

But when Owl arrived at Eclaire's, to share her misery, she found everyone else in a bad mood too. Even Eclaire's big fat cushions and huge plate of cakes didn't seem to lighten the atmosphere. Owl had never seen everyone looking so grumpy at once. Was it just her mood? Or were even the big fat squad of cuddly toys scowling at her?

"Phew," she mumbled, "I th-thought you s-said there was nothing wrong? Has s-somebody died?"

"You look like yesterday's left-overs yourself," said Lizzy crossly, "but at least your hair doesn't look like a mad upside-down beard, like mine."

"Whatever gave you that idea?" Eclaire was amazed. "Anyway, I thought you'd stopped worrying about your hair."

"Huh!" Lizzy snorted. Actually a boy at school had said her hair reminded him of a beard and it had hurt her feelings.

"If all I had to worry about was my hair, I'd be fine," continued Eclaire. "Just try having a mother who keeps buying you clothes three sizes too small and then saying you might shrink into them."

"Just try having a mother who never has enough money to buy you anything at all. I haven't even got a pair of trainers," added Flash. They all looked down at Flash's holey old gym shoes and felt even worse.

"Oh well. I suppose we'd better start," said Eclaire and they gloomily chanted:

"All for one and one for all
Fatty, skinny, short and tall
Frizzy, Flash, Owl and Eclaire
Stick together, foul or fair."

And then they all slumped down in the cushions in a doomy silence broken only by the irritable tapping of fingers and scuffing of shoes on the carpet. Soon, these dismal sounds were joined by another: the faint but audible snuffling of Owl.

Eclaire jumped guiltily. "Oh Owl, I forgot! You're upset about something aren't you? This meeting was meant to be for you! What's up?"

"N-nothing," muttered Owl, sinking her head into her neck behind her huge glasses. She looked more than ever like a baby owl that has just dropped from its nest and knows it will never see a juicy mouse again.

"Oh come on," said Eclaire, offering a vast pink box of tissues and a vast pink comforting arm. Eclaire was swathed in a luminous puce angora sweater which made her blend rather disconcertingly into her army of cuddly toys.

"Yeah Owl, what's up," asked Flash, feeling pleased to forget about her moans and genuinely sorry for Owl, who by now had tears as large as boulders running down her little cheeks.

"Hey Owly, this isn't like you," added Lizzy, pulling a filthy old tissue from her pocket and clumsily attempting to stem the flood of Owl's tears. Owl had shrunk even further into herself at the sight of the pink tissues – they were too big, and soft, and pink for her. Now she shrank further still from Lizzy's kindly offered, but very disgusting one.

"I c-can't," sobbed Owl, resorting to her sleeve to wipe her nose. "I just c-can't. You'll all laugh."

"We won't, we won't, we won't," chorused the trio. "We're your friends, we're here to help."

There was a long painful silence.

"You've helped us – a lot," said Eclaire. "Now we want to help you. Go on Owl, let us."

"I-I've done something really s-stupid," snuffled Owl at last.

"What? You, stupid?" said Eclaire. "You know what a brainbox you are."

"Yeah. If you've done something stupid then I'm a roast potato," chortled Lizzy.

"And I'm a fried banana," added Flash.

"Th-this is serious," said Owl.

"Well tell us then," they all nagged. So she did.

"You see, I-I've b-been l-longing and longing to act and th-there's a p-play on at school and I-I'v-volunteered to audition."

"But Owl that's great! That's what you've always wanted," cheered Eclaire. "You'll knock 'em dead."

"B-b-but it's a musical," sobbed Owl.

"What's wrong with that? You've got a brilliant voice, you know you have."

"B-but I s-said I wanted to be the lead part, y-you know the main character. I can't, I just can't."

"Well, why not? You can sing, you can act. You won't be shy when you're up there. Why not aim for the stars?" Eclaire was really excited now.

"B-but y-you don't know w-what the l-lead part is," stuttered Owl in desperation. "And I c-can't tell you, cos you really will just laugh your heads off."

"Oh come on Owl," said Flash, rather fiercely, "You know better than that. What's the point of having a life's ambition to act if when the opportunity comes up you just run away?"

"B-but if I t-tell you what it is, you'll understand," said Owl.

"WELL, GO ON THEN!" shouted Lizzy.

"You promise not to laugh?"

"We promise."

So Owl whispered to each of them what the part was.

First she whispered to Lizzy, then to Flash, then to Eclaire. And to each of them in turn, the same thing happened. Each of them turned first pink, then red, then their cheeks swelled, then their eyes bulged, then they snorted, then they nearly choked and then they just couldn't help it. All three of Owl's best friends rolled on the floor, convulsed in giggles. Eclaire laughed so much she thought she would die. She looked like a large pink blob from another world, that had sprouted a pair of strange little antennae that waved about in search of food or friendship. In fact these were her legs, kicking helplessly in an attempt to control her mirth. Lizzy roared till the tears streamed down her face. Flash tried to stuff the pink tissues into her mouth in order not to laugh, but unfortunately found herself with a mouthful of Lizzy's revolting one, spat it out and just gave in.

Owl sat quite calmly in the midst of the gale-force laughter. She had known this would happen. And these were her best friends. Imagine how strangers would react.

Gradually, the hoots and cackles subsided. Eclaire, kind as ever, was the first to comfort Owl.

"Owly," she wheedled "I'm sorry. We're all sorry. We're so, so sorry."

Owl sat in stony silence.

"No we are, Owl, we are, we are," chorused Lizzy and Flash.

Owl, if such a thing is possible, became quieter still. Imagine a desolate snowscape in which nothing stirs, not even an ant.

Owl's silence was like that.

Eclaire resorted to poetry. In a swooping but tuneless trill, she warbled:

"Ooooh Owly, Owly,
What are we to dooooo?
We've been so very fouly
Owly, to yoooooooo.
We don't deserve to live!
Can you pleeeeeeease forgive?"

The silence that followed this was different to

Owl's frozen gloom. It was brief, and amazed.

"Did you make that up on the spot?" asked Lizzy.

Eclaire blushed.

Owl had to smile. "I-it's you who should g-go on stage," she said. "You c-could write the stuff as well."

"No, it's you," said Eclaire firmly, taking advantage of Owl's new mood. "I can't sing for toffee." This was certainly true, Eclaire's voice was the kind that makes music teachers ask children to mime during concerts.

"Yes, of course it's you Owly," added Lizzy "Can you imagine Eclaire actually singing on stage?"

"Owl, if you're scared of the lead, how about a smaller part?" Flash suggested.

"Oh. You think I'm like a hamster too," Owl retorted. Since no one understood this remark, they all continued to try to persuade Owl not to give up.

"No. Owl should go for the lead," said Eclaire,

adding, "I know we all laughed at first, but people often play against type. You don't have to be tall or blond to play a tall blonde person any more. Theatre isn't about that. It's about acting."

"Yeah," added Flash, "like, you know, when big hairy men play the Ugly Sisters and girls play boys..."

"That's panto," said Owl squashingly, "and everyone's supposed to laugh at that."

"No, but Flash is right," said Lizzy. "You often see really good actors playing something that if you just saw their photo, you wouldn't think would suit them at all."

"And they use make-up, and wigs," enthused Eclaire.

"And stilts?" Owl interrupted.

"Oh don't be such a grump," Lizzy was quite cross. "We're here to help you. Come on Owl, you may be shy, but you're not a coward. I think you should give this one everything you've got."

"Yeah. Reach for the stars! Nothing ventured, nothing gained," added Flash.

☆ 23 ☆

"You can't be brave unless you're scared in the first place," said Lizzy. "People who aren't frightened and worried just lumber on through life not noticing anything. But if you're scared and you still do it, then that's something to be really proud of."

Owl thought about this.

"OK, I will give it a go," she said finally "but I'm g-gonna need a lot of help."

"Owl! You're a star already," whooped Eclaire, hugging her. "Now, what you should do, is learn the whole part by heart, so that when it comes to the audition all you'll have to worry about is the expression and feelings, you know, cos the lines will just come easily. Don't you agree Owl? Owl?"

There was no reply. This was because Owl was nearly suffocated by Eclaire's enormous bear hug.

A vast bowl of chips and a few glasses of Toxic Melon (one of Eclaire's strange, but delicious, home-made potions) had a mildly reviving effect on the Fab Four, who ended their meeting rather more cheerfully than they had begun it.

They all agreed to take turns coaching Owl and listening to her lines, and all ended the meeting with a heartfelt chant:

"Four for one and one for four
Funny, clever, rich and poor
Frizzy, Flash, Eclaire and Owl
Stick together, fair or foul."

And they parted with a rousing shout of "Meringue!"

"Course," muttered Lizzy to Flash as they left "She hasn't got a bat's chance in hell of getting the part."

"Oh. I don't know," laughed Flash. "Pigs might fly... why shouldn't a mute midget play a Giant Warrior Queen of the Ice Maidens?"

☆ 25 ☆

☆ CHAPTER THREE ☆

During the next week Lizzy, Flash and Eclaire did their best to drown their doubts and put all their energy into helping Owl learn her part.

Eclaire took it upon herself to teach Owl to relax. She had a book of breathing exercises and she went through it every day with Owl, showing her how to breathe deeply to feel calmer.

"Is th-this why you're always s-so c-calm and cheerful yourself?" asked Owl after one of their sessions.

"Me? Calm?" giggled Eclaire. "D'you really think so?"

As she said this, she glowed with satisfaction, breathed in deeply and breathed out, bursting three buttons on her capacious angora cardigan.

Flash decided that her best way to help Owl was exercise. She gave her a little list of simple press-ups and arm swinging things to loosen her up.

"It's important to move well on stage you know," she said earnestly "It's not just your voice and the words you know, it's the whole you. You've got to like, think yourself into the part. Become a Warrior Queen. Feel tall."

"I know," muttered Owl. "But you're so super fit and sporty – I'll never be like you."

"Am I?" said Flash, looking smug.

'And dead bossy, too', thought Owl. 'Still,' she pondered mournfully, "it's better than having no personality at all, like me...'

Still, she religiously did her deep breathing and her arm swings every morning and every evening before Lizzy came round to coach her with her lines. Lizzy was unusually patient at listening to her and rather good at giving her tips on expression. She also persuaded Owl to speak as loudly as possible by the rather clever ruse of holding her hands over her ears.

"C'mon, speak UP! I can't HEAR you," she would shout. And this caused Owl to raise her voice first to a whisper, then to a murmur, then to a mutter, then to a conversational tone and finally to something nearly like a proper actor's voice which has to carry to the back of a theatre. During one of these sessions, Loretta burst into Owl's bedroom.

"Em! Was that you? It sounded amazing!"

"N-no. It was Lizzy," stuttered Owl in dismay. "I'm l-listening to her rehearse for the school play."

"Lizzy, you're a brilliant mimic. You sound exactly like Em," laughed Loretta. "Or at least like she would sound if she ever dared speak above a whisper. Stupid of me really, cos she never even dares say 'hello' to the milkman so I can't imagine how she'd ever do anything like acting! See ya." And tall beautiful Loretta swept out, leaving Owl with a very big smile on her face.

"You see?" said Lizzy. "You can do it. It's just a question of confidence to do it in front of someone who isn't your best friend."

"Yes," thought Owl. "I can. I CAN do it. I know that. But do I DARE do it?" This was a question, she felt, that would only be answered at the audition. "Please, please, make it me... please, please, make it me," she whispered, over and over.

Two days later, Owl was word perfect. Four days after that, she had all of the Fab Four in stitches while she strutted about draped in an old sheet as the Giant Warrior Queen of the Ice Maidens. She was funny, she was frightening, she could sing like a lark.

"You'll get the part, absolutely no doubt about it." This was Flash's conclusion and the others agreed.

Even Owl began to think they were right. But the words kept running through her head: "I CAN do it. But do I DARE?"

On the day of the audition, Owl woke with such mixed feelings of dread and excitement that she found it impossible to eat a thing for breakfast.

"Breakfast is brain food," said her mother sternly. "Eat in the morning and you'll be clever all day." Mrs Smith worried herself silly over her shy younger daughter. She seemed to have spent her whole life thinking that Emily would grow out of it. When little Em had clung to her at playgroup the other mothers had said, "Oh, they're all like that to begin with, don't you worry, she'll grow out of it." At infants school the other mothers had said, "Oh, they're all like that to begin with, don't you worry, she'll grow out of it." But while other shy children had grown out of it, Em never had. She just couldn't understand it. But one thing made her very proud: her little Emily had a very big brain. And that was why she talked about brain food. She thought that if Em was going to be so shy all her life then she might as well at least be clever. Perhaps it would make her less shy eventually... hoped Mrs Smith.

But this morning her words had no effect. Owl was stupefied with fear, and to eat anything would undoubtedly make her sick. Her mother sighed to herself as she watched her little daughter trailing off to school. So small, and so, so, shy. Where, wondered Mrs Smith, had she gone wrong?

Unaware of her mother's worries, Owl was so nervous about the audition that she considered taking the day off school. She knew kids who did that. They just went to the park for the day and came back at tea time and their mothers never knew the difference. But Owl didn't like the idea. First, you never knew who you might meet in the park. Second, if she was discovered, her mother would be really upset. Third – and most important – she couldn't face the Fab Four if she didn't go to the audition.

In the audition room, Owl's worst fears were confirmed. All the girls waiting seemed to be

about eight feet taller than she was. They all had big blonde hair, big bouncy chests and big booming voices. They were like models or actresses, not like schoolgirls at all. She was sure they were laughing at her. She could hear sniggers. But she sat down, clenched her teeth and decided she wouldn't look up until her name was called. As she watched the others go in, one by one, she realised even their names sounded like actresses' names: one was called Zinnia Heart! Another, Gloria Sky! Yet another, Dolores Azores!

Owl resigned herself to the fact that the fates were against her. She had known she was in a big school, but she hadn't noticed till now that it housed quite so many goddesses as this...

To her relief, she heard a quite ordinary sounding name being called. She looked up to see if there was an ordinary looking person to whom it belonged – and then she realised it was her own.

"Emily Smith!" repeated the Ironglove's voice from behind the door. Owl shot to her feet. Then, for one glorious second, she considered just running away. She could zip out the back way, cut through the playground and be in the park in two minutes flat... But the Ironglove's vast head had appeared in the doorway, and there was little doubt that the Ironglove's vast body would soon follow it. There was no escape.

As Owl took the long walk (which was actually about 3.2 seconds) from her bench to the door, these words kept running through her head: "I CAN do it. But do I DARE? I CAN do it. But do I DARE? I CAN do it. But do I DARE?"

As she stumbled on the carpet and fell into the rehearsal room she was shocked to see three other people sitting behind the Ironglove. They were Mrs Spindle the music teacher. Mr Thoroughgood, the dance teacher. And last but not least, the appalling figure of Mr Vim, the PE teacher. To say that Mr Vim was unpopular would be to understate the case. There were children at the school who would rather be put in a cage of hungry tigers than spend time with Mr Vim. Finding excuses to avoid his lessons was the best exercise most of his pupils got. Their hands ached from forging notes excusing themselves from his classes. The paper expended on these notes alone must have wasted several forests,

'Why on earth was he here?' thought Owl.

"This is Emily Smith," said Mrs Ironglove, in

her kindest voice. Mrs Ironglove's kindest voice reminded Em of a crocodile shouting, but Mrs Ironglove was, in fact, quite a kind person and a good drama teacher. She couldn't help her voice, Owl supposed. And also Owl supposed that that was the reason she taught drama rather than practising it. There can't be that many parts outside pantomime for people whose voices sound like a crocodile...

"Emily, you know Mrs Spindle, who will be doing our music, and Mr Thoroughgood of course, who is helping me choose the best, um movers for the chorus, and er, Mr Vim," (the Ironglove sounded apologetic) who has ... kindly volunteered to help with the fight scenes. We don't want anyone to hurt themselves, do we?" The Ironglove roared a raucous crocodile cackle and Owl shot Mr Vim a nervous glance. His expression seemed to say "Oh? Don't we?"

Mrs Ironglove glanced at Owl and then at Mr Vim. She couldn't imagine the shy little girl lasting five seconds with this huge, bossy man. Still, she had to admit it was obvious little Emily Smith wouldn't get the part. Mrs Ironglove felt a wave of sympathy wash over her – she remembered auditioning herself, when she was about this girl's age, and being told she sounded like a crocodile.

'Such experiences can be very damaging,' thought Mrs Ironglove.

"Come on Emily," she said briskly. "I'd like you to read the speech where the Giant Warrior Queen of the Ice Maidens is declaring war on the Fiendish Dragon King of the Goblins... it's on page 16..."

"I-I know th-that bit already," whispered Owl, her head throbbing as if a herd of elephants were gallumphing through it.

"You've learnt it? Excellent! Go ahead then."

Owl breathed deeply as Eclaire had shown her. Unfortunately she breathed in a passing fly and the next two minutes were spent being thumped

on the back by the vast Mr Vim and having a glass of water thrown over her by Mrs Ironglove.

"I'm SO sorry, dear," bellowed the Ironglove, "I tripped over Mr Vim's karate belt." She glared at Mr Vim. "I meant you to drink the water."

"I-I've swallowed it," Owl gasped, horrified.

"I know an old ladeeee who swallowed a fly," trilled Mrs Spindle, in a clumsy attempt to cheer things up.

☆ **39** ☆

"Now dear, do you think you could manage?" asked Mrs Ironglove, in an even kinder voice than before.

"I th-think so," Owl repeated to herself: breathe deeply (Done that, bad mistake); open eyes (She checked. Yup, she could see Mr Vim glowering at her, so her eyes must be open); head up (Was her head up? She was so small it was hard to tell); last, most important, speak UP!

"Oh vile King! Whose demons plague my bowl, sorry, soul..." she ground to a halt.

"Is there a baby grasshopper in the room?" asked Mr Vim with what he thought was a cheeky wit. "Or was that a girl speaking?"

Mrs Ironglove gave him a frosty glare.

"Have another glass of water dear. Yes, drink it this time."

"Why not try one of the songs?" added Mrs Spindle. "The Queen has two very important songs, so it's essential that anyone who plays her can sing, dear."

"Good idea. Do the one where she swears her

love for the King of the Sun," said Mrs Ironglove encouragingly, hoping against hope that poor little Emily would be able to sing.

Owl knew she could sing beautifully. She was determined to give it her best go:

"Oh Orlando, Oh Sun King
I've loved you from the start..."

(Owl felt rising excitement as she saw all four teachers leaning forward with eager expressions. She was singing perfectly.)

"...Oh Orlando, Oh Sun King
Only you could melt my fart..."

Oh no! Was it possible she had sung that? Was it possible? There was a shocked silence.

"I suppose you think that's amusing," said Mr Vim, raising himself to his full, terrifying height.

"N-no, n-no n-o. I'm s-so sorry," wailed Owl, bursting into tears and making for the door.

To her terror, she felt a hand on her shoulder. To her amazement she realised that Mrs Ironglove was looking at her very kindly. The reason for this, though Owl was never to know, was that Mrs Ironglove had made a very similar mistake herself once, in the very same audition in which she had been told she sounded like a crocodile.

"See me later," she said, looking deep into Owl's streaming eyes.

Later that afternoon, Mrs Ironglove called all the young hopefuls to a meeting. The part of the Giant Warrior Queen of the Ice Maidens was given to Dolores Azores, the tallest, strongest, prettiest, blondest, loudest girl of all. The Queen's handmaidens were all to be played by tall, confident girls too.

Mrs Ironglove, meanwhile, had been thinking about Owl. She had been thinking about that audition long ago when she had muddled her words up. It's true that all she had said was "poo tarts," when she should have said "two parts," but it had been bad enough in her day. Almost as bad as saying "Fart," instead of "Heart." The Ironglove saw it as her mission to rescue Owl from the same disappointment.

"There are still a few parts we have not cast," she said. "Emily, you have a lovely singing voice: would you like to be the Magic Tree Stump?"

A gaggle of giggles swept the room.

"That's enough!" shouted Mrs Ironglove. "The part of the tree stump is an exceedingly important one, as any of you who have bothered to read the play will know. Some people, like brave little Emily here, have read it – and even bothered to learn some of it."

Owl felt hot and bothered. Actually she had only read the words of the Giant Warrior Queen of the Ice Maidens and had no idea about the Magic Tree Stump. She was embarrassed, and certain that the Ironglove was trying to make her feel even worse by actually offering her a part as some scenery. She wondered what it felt like to be eaten slowly by red ants. Not worse than this, surely?

"Well, if you won't take my word for it, read the play. The little tree stump plays a vital role in the marriage of the Ice Queen," glared Mrs Ironglove at the big, laughing girls and boys. "Think about it, Emily."

And with that, Mrs Ironglove dismissed the gathering.

☆ (HAPTER FOUR ☆

Owl wasn't sure she could face the Fab Four, who
had, of course, arranged to meet that night to
discuss the audition. But since the meeting was at
her house, she felt she couldn't really get out of it.
Dismally she poured four glasses of flat lemonade
and scattered the remains of a packet of biscuits
onto a plate. There were two biscuits and a lot of
crumbs, obviously Loretta had been at the packet
first. What did it matter? The meeting wouldn't
be long...

Dismally, Owl trudged upstairs. Dismally, she
moved the goldfish bowl so that there would be

room for the others to crowd in under the tiny bunk bed. Dismally, she trudged up and down stairs letting them all in. She had never felt so unlike a jolly meeting in her life.

One glance at the mournful face that greeted them had shown each of the others that Owl was not heading for an Oscar.

But Lizzy made an effort and opened the meeting with the usual chant and cries of, "Meringue."

"OK Owl? How'd it go?" she asked in a fake bouncy voice.

"Oh it was great," said Owl, in a voice like a suicidal bee.

"OK. You didn't get it. Who did? Shall we poison her?" said Flash.

"Dolores Azores, of course," muttered Owl.

"Maybe you could be one of the other ice maidens?" said Eclaire, immediately wishing she hadn't spoken.

"Actually," said Owl, "I was offered a part."

"Owl! That's great! What was it?"

"A tree stump."

"You're joking," Flash was lost for words.

"That's a disgrace. That's a real insult. I'm going to write and complain. How can a great actress like you be a tree stump?" shouted Lizzy.

"Oh Owl! That's outrageous. I am sorry," said Eclaire, bundling Owl up in her pink woolly embrace.

"Yes," said Owl, more angry than sad now, "and she actually had the nerve to say it was an important part! Can you believe it? S-something about without the tree stump, the queen would never get to marry the k-king!"

"Oh yeah? And who does the tree stump marry?" snorted Flash.

"Wait a minute, wait a minute," said Lizzy, who suddenly remembered a bit of the play she had read while helping Owl with her lines. "I think the tree stump is quite important. Owl, get the play."

"Oh d-don't t-try to be kind. How c-can a t-tree stump be important?" Owl snuffled.

"No Owl, I'm serious," said Lizzy. "Get the play, let's have a look."

It was easy for all four girls to read the play at once, as they were so tightly huddled together.

"See?" said Owl, as it soon became clear that the tree stump did not have a speaking part.

"But wait," said Eclaire. "It does sing."

And indeed it did. The Magic Tree Stump

turned out, in fact, to have a central part in the whole drama.

It started life at the beginning of the play as a young oak tree, which is cut down by the nasty vulcans. It sings a mournful little plea for its life, and the life of all trees on our beautiful planet (joined by a chorus of fluting wood elves and squirrels), before the vicious axe falls and silences it, apparently forever.

"So that's all?" said Owl, slightly interested in the tragedy of the little tree despite herself.

"No, look," squeaked Eclaire, hardly able to contain her excitement. "Later it's got a really important thing to do, just like your teacher said! The brave little tree stump trips up the wicked Emperor of the Vulcans just as he is about to kidnap the Warrior Queen!"

"Yes," said Lizzy, "and it sends the emperor hurtling into a ravine, so that the King of the Sun can whisk off the Giant Warrior Queen to Happiness Ever After."

They read on: at the end of the play, the tree

stump sings a triumphant ditty about the revenge of the trees, and how even as stumps they can be useful and about how humanity and nature should be in oneness with the universe and combining to help each other.

"Well fancy that," said Eclaire, looking on the bright side as usual. "In a way, the tree stump is the hero of the whole play."

"It's true," added Lizzy. "You don't have to speak to be important. You ought to know that yourself Owly."

"Sure, look at Charlie Chaplin or Buster Keaton or... or... Mr Bean!"

"Yeah. And it really gives you a brilliant chance to show what a great singing voice you have," said Flash.

Owl wondered whether Mrs Ironglove had noticed that she had sung a couple of lines really well, until she'd made that ghastly mistake. She may have sounded like a vole with laryngitis when she spoke, but when she sang she had, even she had to admit, been rather good.

"Of course you must do it Owl. It's a great opportunity," said Flash.

"It would have been really scary to be the Giantess Queen Thingy, this will be miles better to start off on."

Owl was perking up. She suddenly remembered that Mrs Ironglove had said she had a lovely singing voice... Maybe she had meant it. It would have been really scary to play the Warrior Queen. She had to admit she might have felt the teensiest bit daft being a quarter the size of her handmaidens...

"You're right," she said. "I'll do it!"

The Fab Four (well, three of them) crowded round. Owl felt better than she had for weeks.

Owl spent the rest of the evening and far into the night learning the tree stump songs. Even though she had got the part, she didn't want to risk looking stupid again. She now wanted to play the Magic Tree Stump more than anything on earth. She knew she could sing. And the big advantage of playing a tree was that she'd be covered from top to toe in twigs, so no one would know it was her. That night, for the first night in weeks, she slept like a, well, like a log.

It wasn't until the lunch break next day that Owl could track down Mrs Ironglove.

"Th-thankyou for offering me the p-part," she said. "I would like to do it. V-very very m-much."

The expression on Mrs Ironglove's face was not what Owl had hoped for. She looked like a wet weekend.

"But dear, it's gone."

Owl realised that the Ironglove must think she meant the Queen's part.

"N-no, not the qu-qu-qu-queen. You know, the tree stump," said Owl.

Mrs Ironglove composed her features to form the kind of expression adults wear when they have something very bad to tell you and don't quite know how.

"I'm afraid I've given the part of the tree stump to little Brian Hayseed dear. You see, you didn't seem at all interested yesterday, and he wanted it so very, very much. Didn't you dear?" she concluded, turning to little Brian Hayseed, who was standing by her elbow.

"Yeah. Cos it would be wicked to trip up Damien," chortled Brian.

Damien Hogwurt, who was about nine feet tall and seven feet wide, was playing the wicked Emperor of the Vulcans. Owl agreed it would be wicked to trip him up. There was nothing more to say. Owl had failed to seize the opportunity when she had it – and now it had gone.

Suddenly, she wanted to be in the play more than anything. Was there no part she could play? Not a squirrel? A wood elf? "How about a t-t-toadstool?" she asked desperately.

"No, the toadstools are being played by smaller, um, I mean, younger children," said Mrs

Ironglove. "But it would be wonderful if you could be Brian's understudy – and wouldn't you like to help with the costumes and scenery? That would be marvellous! You're so good with your hands, such lovely little hands..."

Flash was the first to arrive at Owl's house that evening. She was horrified to find Owl furiously tearing up her theatre posters.

"Owl! You can't! It's the love of your life! Don't be so BABY-ish!"

Stung by this rebuke, Owl stopped. She told Flash all that had happened.

"Well, it is tough," admitted Flash, "but you can't expect to have something just fall into your lap. You've never even tried to be in a play before. And if you love theatre so much, why don't you learn about it by doing scenery and stuff. It's not all about being a star."

"You don't understand, it's n-not happening to you," grumbled Owl.

"Oh no? And don't I spend hours every week

ₒ out stables just so I can get a chance to ₔide an old pony now and then? I don't go around weeping and wailing cos I'm not showjumping at Olympia."

"That's different. You've never d-done any j-jumping."

"And you, Owl, if you don't mind me saying, have never done any acting. It's all in your head."

"B-but I know I c-can do it. I know I can!," sobbed Owl. "I don't want to just m-mess about with stupid costumes!"

"I'd have thought it would be more fun than shovelling horse manure," sneered Flash, feeling really furious with Owl for the first time. "You just think you're above it. And you're not."

It was at this moment Eclaire and Lizzy arrived, having been let in by Loretta.

"Flash, you're being horrible," said kind Eclaire, threatening to suffocate Owl once more in her embrace. Today, she had a purple woolly top with yellow satin bananas and pineapples on the front. Owl wasn't sure she could face being

engulfed in a fruit salad. She ducked. Eclaire went flying, tearing down the last theatre poster in an attempt to save herself before hurtling into the goldfish bowl. The little creature's life was saved by Flash, who, quick as a flash, dived for the bowl before its entire contents had spilled. Several minutes were passed refilling the bowl, checking the small fish was not hurt, topping up its minute amount of feed – and, inevitably, apologising to each other.

"I think Flash is right," said Lizzy finally, when they had all settled. "If you really love theatre Owl – and not just the idea of being a star, why don't you give it a go? Lots of people started off as stage managers…"

"Or you might turn out to be a great designer," added Eclaire. "Designers are just as important as actors, they don't get so much credit, that's all…"

"You know? You all sound like headmistresses," scowled Owl. "But I suppose I'll give it a go. It won't be hard making Brian look like a tree stump – he's even smaller than m-me and has very sprouty hair… like twigs."

"Anyway," said Flash mischievously, "maybe he'll be ill on the night."

This put ideas into everyone's heads. But nobody said anything.

The next couple of weeks saw all the girls helping out Owl in her new found career. They collected bark and twigs and even helped her in the laborious process of cutting out and painting two hundred oak leaves for the wood scene. It'll help cheer her up, they thought to themselves, for they had truly never seen Owl so low.

Owl began almost to enjoy making the props and learning more about backstage stuff. She got fond of Mrs Ironglove, who was always encouraging about her contribution.

"You know Em," said Mrs Ironglove one day. "You're a girl of many talents. You can sing, you can paint, there's no need to be quiet as a mouse."

But still, every night, Owl would stand in front of the bathroom mirror, mouthing to herself the whole of the Warrior Queen's part. One day... one day... it shall be me! Make it me!

Lizzy, Eclaire and Flash meanwhile, met in their own school at lunchtime and plotted. They had to get tickets for Owl's play, they decided, and give her all the support they possibly could.

"We've all got to shout at the end for the designers," said Flash, "So that Owl can come on and take a curtain call."

"Hmmm... That might be an idea, but is it enough? Isn't there anything else we could do?" wondered Lizzy.

"If only little Brian Hayseed could have something wrong with him. Nothing too serious," joked Flash. "Just a little honey fungus or Dutch elm disease."

"Well, there's the obvious..." twinkled Eclaire mischievously.

The obvious, according to Eclaire, was to murder poor little Brian Hayseed – and that sort of thing only happened in thrillers. No, it wouldn't do, they agreed.

"I know," said Flash suddenly. "I'll ring up just before he's due to go on and say there's an emergency at home."

"Like what?" Lizzy was sarcastic. "Anyway, his folks will be at the play, won't they?"

"If we kidnapped him, just for a little while, and were very nice to him, you know, gave him sweeties and all..." murmured Eclaire thoughtfully.

"We'd end up in some vile Place of Correction for Young Offenders. Don't be daft," said Lizzy, realistic as ever. "But, um," she added, "You might be on to something about giving him sweets..."

"You mean poison him?" asked Eclaire, shocked.

"No... just too many sweets, you know, combined with pre-stage nerves. That might do the trick."

"Brilliant," said Eclaire. "I'll make him some of my specially gooey chocwhizzers..."

"Yeah," laughed Flash. "It's worth a try. They're doing a dress rehearsal earlier on the day of the performance. We'll go along to 'help' Owl, and stuff him with as many sicky sweets as poss."

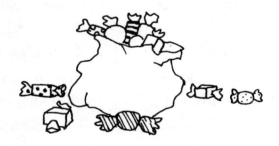

☆ CHAPTER FIVE ☆

Eventually the big day came. Flash, Eclaire and Lizzy all met up at the backstage door of the school hall. They were very early, but armed with bagfulls of disgustingly sickly goodies for poor little Brian. And sure enough, the innocent little chap was a willing victim.

"Hey Brian, let me help you with the costume," said Eclaire, charmingly "Oh, and would you like some of my special toffee Munchettes?"

"Oh Brian, let me rearrange your twigs," wheedled Flash, cramming Brian's willing hands with Fudgemallows. "Here's a few more for your pockets," she added, "acting is hungry work."

"Shall I pop a few of these in your mouth for you?" murmured Lizzy, proffering Iced Kola drops "Only I know it's hard to do it yourself with those branches."

"Mmmmm... hmmm... unghhh," muttered Brian, gratefully, as he tottered on stage, hoovering up more and more sweets.

"Reminds me of feeding a hamster," said Lizzy. "Just snuffles it all up into his pouches. D'you think his parents deprived him of sweets when he was little?"

"He is little. He might make it through the dress rehearsal, but he'll be a gonner by the time of the show," gloated Eclaire.

But just to be on the safe side, they left a whole bag of nuclear nougat. "For the interval. Good luck, Brian," waved Lizzy cheerfully, as they left, cackling with glee.

Two hours later they met again, this time outside the front of the hall. The place was packed with twittering parents, thrilled at the prospect of their little darlings waltzing about dressed as robins and dwarves.

"Are all the actors OK?" Lizzy asked a tall pimply youth selling programmes.

"Fraid not," said the youth.

Eclaire's heart leapt. "OH? Is one of them ill?" she asked hopefully.

"No," smirked the youth "They just can't act. Heh, heh."

"Oh, very funny," sniffed Flash and strode down the aisle to her seat, dragging Eclaire and Lizzy in her wake.

As they took their seats in the hall, they noticed that both Owl's parents and her sister Loretta were in the front row.

"They're so pleased she's got involved in something," whispered Lizzy.

"Yeah," laughed Flash. "Her mum said it's the first time she's ever taken part in anything involving more than one person – even a conversation!"

"Oh look!" whispered Lizzy. "Owl's got her name in the programme!" And there it was: co-designer Emily Smith.

"Phew, makes you proud," murmured Flash.

"Oh GREAT," said Eclaire. "My Dad and your Mum have made it."

Lizzy looked round, pleased. The more people who could cheer for the designer the better, she felt.

As the lights dimmed, the three girls were on the edges of their rickety old chairs. Supposing the scenery collapsed? Supposing the papier mâché toadstools Owl had been up all night making fell apart? Supposing the squirrels' tails got caught in the vulcans' headdresses as they scampered about in the branches above, throwing down their nuts? Supposing Dolores Azores's silver dungarees fell down? This last thought caused Eclaire to laugh so much she nearly toppled over the whole row of chairs. Rows of furious parents turned to glare.

"Good luck Owl, this is for you," whispered Eclaire, with her fingers crossed and hoping against hope that it would all go smoothly.

Owl, meanwhile, was flapping about backstage helping everyone with their costumes, sewing on leaves, adjusting squirrels' tails, comforting wood elves afflicted with stage fright. She had hardly any time to think, until she heard the first sounds of the school orchestra playing the opening tune. The play was starting, and she wasn't in it. She sat down on a little tree stump to cry, only noticing at the last moment that it was Brian Hayseed she was sitting on.

"Oh Brian, I'm so sorry. I thought you were a real tree stump."

"What would a real tree stump be doing backstage?" asked Brian huffily, ruffling his twigs. Poor Owl spent the next few minutes blinking back her tears as she helped Brian into the top part of his costume and rearranged her rival's leaves for his big moment.

"I didn't hurt you, did I Brian?" Owl asked, suddenly hopeful. She noticed that it wasn't just Brian's leaves that were looking green...

The curtain rose…

To the great disappointment of Lizzy, Flash and Eclaire, little Brian Hayseed appeared solidly as the tree. He couldn't sing half as well as Owl, but he did look awfully sweet with his little twiggy hair, his large round eyes gazing soulfully through twin peepholes in his bark and his tiny stumpy legs encased in a trunk suit.

"He must have a stomach lined with lead," hissed Flash, "we should have put some laxative in the fudge."

Dolores Azores, it had to be admitted, was magnificent as the Giant Warrior Queen of the Ice Maidens. Majestic in silver dungarees and a viking helmet with wings, she stormed about the stage like a hurricane. Her huge voice filled the old school hall, her enormous hair swirled like a gleaming thundercloud about her magnificently proportioned brow. Both she and Brian got a big round of applause: Brian for his tragic little plea for his life as the fiendish Vulcan Warriors chopped him down – Dolores for her superb operatic song about saving nature from the vulcan hordes.

In the interval Lizzy, Eclaire and Flash crowded round Owl with congratulations.

"How on earth did you get that tree costume to fall in half like that when they cut him down? It was amazing."

"Yeah, I thought Brian's head was gonna come off," laughed Flash.

"Shame it didn't," added Lizzy.

"Oh, thanks," muttered Owl, miserably. She felt touched by their support, but all she wanted was to be on stage herself. Was she destined forever to only be good at something she didn't want to do?

But, to Owl's horror, when she went backstage again three minutes before it was time for the curtain to rise for the second act, little Brian Hayseed was nowhere to be seen! His little stump costume stood in the middle of the stage, empty.

'It looks so lonely sitting there, waiting for him,' thought Owl. 'And this was his big scene, his 'wicked' moment to trip the Vulcan Emperor!

Terrible fantasies rushed through Owl's head. Supposing one of the fab Four had kidnapped him? She would never live it down! They wouldn't, would they? Or had she hurt him when she sat on him? But she had no time to think, there were only seconds to spare. Mrs Ironglove was insisting that Owl go on and be the stump.

"Go on! Get into the costume, quickly!" she ordered.

"I c-can't," Owl cried, suddenly terrified.

"Emily," said Mrs Ironglove very sternly indeed, "You are the understudy. That is what understudies DO. They take over when someone fails to turn up."

"I know b-but what about B-Brian?" quivered Owl.

"Oh, don't worry, he's sure to turn up in the end. Probably just stage fright," said Mrs Ironglove more kindly.

'Stage fright, that's definitely what I'm suffering from,' thought Owl. But she knew she had to do it. She had said 'no' once too often. She scrambled into the stump costume, dizzy with terror.

The orchestra struck up – a high pitched screech of violins and flutes attempting to emulate wind and owls.

The curtain rose on the moonlit tree stump. And in it, was Owl.

'How peculiar,' thought Owl. 'Here I am, on stage, in a real play for the first time in my life, and nobody knows it's me. All they can see is a little tree stump and they think that inside is little Brian Hayseed, cos that's what it says in the programme. And even his mother won't know the difference until I sing. And when they hear my voice, they'll just laugh, cos it doesn't sound a bit like Brian's.'

But she didn't have much time to think further, because on came Damien Hogwurt, looking ten foot tall in his purple wings and black and silver armour, wielding a knobkerry.

"Ho! Where art thou Warrior Queen?" boomed Damien. "I have come to carry thee off to the volcanic pits where we shall raise a master race of Ice Vulcans to conquer the World. Har har har! Hee, hee, hee! AAARRRGGHHHH!"

And Damien, Emperor of the Vulcans, tripped over the noble tree stump, hurtling over a cliff, never to be seen again. The audience burst into wild applause.

Owl swelled with pride inside her stump. They were applauding her. They didn't know they were applauding her, of course, they thought they were applauding little Brian Hayseed, but still, they were applauding her and it felt very good to Owl. Very good indeed.

Even so, her moment of joy was short.

She became aware that one of the wood elves was squeaking into her twigs.

"Sumfink terrible's 'appened. The Queen of the Ice Maidens 'as 'urt 'er uncle. She can't come on!"

"Hurt her uncle! What are you talking about?" exclaimed Owl, her mind hurtling in several directions at once.

"You know sprained it," whispered the elf feverishly.

"Oh, her ankle," said Owl.

"Thasssss what I said," hissed the elf.

'Oh no!' thought Owl. 'The whole play will be ruined.'

Already the King of the Sun had appeared, singing his duet, the opening lines of which were:

"I have searched the woods and valleys
for my maiden of ice,
And now, my lovely, at last I have
found you..."

There was a seemingly endless silence as he realised the queen had not appeared. Without knowing what she was doing, Owl sprung up out of the tree stump. Her old white dungarees that had been suitable for stage managing, were exactly like the ice queen's, especially since they were streaked with silver spray paint, as was her hair, from spraying all the backcloths just moments before the play started.

The audience gasped as she sung in a beautiful soprano:

"Do not fear my love, it is I,
disguised as a treeeeeeee.
I come, I fly, my love, to theeeeee.
The magic may deceive your eyes
But soon I'll be my normal size!"

And then, without having time to feel fear, Owl went straight into the love song duet that she had sung to her mirror every day for six weeks and which was as familiar to her as her own name.

The moonlit wood scene was so dim, and Owl so convincingly sang the song, that the audience couldn't quite believe their eyes.

How had the Warrior Queen of the Ice Maidens magically transformed herself?

"Who's doing the special effects?" whispered various members of the audience. "They could get a job in the West End..."

"It's Owl!" gasped Flash, Eclaire, Lizzy, Loretta and Mr and Mrs Smith simultaneously. The curtain swooped down again, just in time for the tearful Dolores Azores to limp on and drape herself over the throne for the final act.

Owl became the tree stump again and sung her
haunting little ditty as Dolores and the King of
the Sun gazed tenderly into each others' eyes and
all the squirrels, wood elves, handmaidens to the
Ice Maiden and squires to the King of the Sun,
threw confetti at the loving couple and the brave
Little Tree.

"This is my moment," hissed Owl to herself
and she sung her heart out:

"Though I'm but a little Tree
I have tried to play my part
And I hope you will agree
I've done so with all my heart.
For though they cut me to the quick
The vulcans are destroyed
And now the sad and sick
will soon be overjoyed.

For Sun and Ice together
Our King and Queen will be
For ever and forever
Defenders of the Tree!

And now our play has ended
but our story's just begun
For nature we've befriended
so we all can live as one."

At this glorious moment the whole cast of little bird, elves, squirrels, toadstools, handmaidens and flowers joined in with a rousing chorus:

"SO WEEEE AAAALLLL CAN LIIIIVE
AS ONE-NE-NE-NE-NNE!"

The cast took SIX curtain calls. On the third one, Dolores limped forward and took Owl's little stubby branch in her hand, forcing her to bow as well. To Owl's great relief, Brian appeared from the wings, to take another bow. He was a very leaf-like green, having been violently sick after the excitement of his success in act one.

Brian squeezed Owl's branch too, in gratitude. Damien patted her on the head with his knobkerry – rather too hard, as it turned out– poor Owl tottered, fell over a toadstool and landed in the orchestra pit on top of the double bass player. The noise of the poor double bass player's bow as it wheezed across the strings reminded everyone of a magnified burp. Laughter joined the applause as Owl bravely dusted herself off and climbed back on stage. The King of the Sun (an outrageously handsome boy with golden curls and eyes like a tiger) blew her a kiss.

On the fourth curtain call Mr Vim strode onto the stage. There was a hushed gasp from those in the audience who knew him (which was most of them, of course) and from all of the cast. Help! What had they done now? He shot his arm out in a terrifying gesture – but, to everyone's amazement, his outstretched hand was clasping four huge bouquets of flowers placed in it by Mrs Spindle. They were for the King, Queen, Emperor and brave Little Tree. Mr Vim very carefully split the fourth bouquet in two and handed one half to little Brian and the other to Owl. The two diminutive trees stood blinking shyly in the dazzling lights.

☆ CHAPTER SIX ☆

Two days later the Fab Four had a meeting to celebrate Owl's success. They all brought something to eat and stuffed themselves with meringues, eclairs, doughnuts and nuclear nougat.

"I j-just want to th-thank you all for making me do it," said Owl finally.

"You did it yourself," said Eclaire. "We just kind of stopped you not doing it." ('And a little more besides, but we won't go into that', she thought).

"The thing is, what I've realised," continued Owl, "is that I've always been really shy..."

"No!" said Flash "Really? We hadn't noticed."

"You don't say! You could have knocked me down with a feather," laughed Eclaire. "If you had a feather the size of the Empire State building that is..."

Owl pretended not to notice and continued, "...and on stage, well, I had butterflies and all that, and my heart was g-galloping and my b-brain was humming, but it felt different. I knew I could do it. Do you understand?" Owl stopped, feeling slightly embarrassed at the length of her speech.

"I think so," ventured Lizzy. "It means that while you're acting, you can forget about being shy and just be someone else for a while... like a kind of rest from being you."

"Yes," said Owl excitedly "That's just it."

"Well, as long as you go on being yourself too, Owly," said Eclaire.

"Cos no one in our continent
is quite as good as Owl
For tripping on a consonant
or stumbling on a vowel
And if you upped away and went
Then we would surely howl!"

"Eclaire!" said Lizzy, astonished. "You didn't just make that up, did you?"

"Um, no, I wrote it last night," murmured Eclaire.

"Wish you'd written the school play," mumbled Owl.

It was the first time any of them had admitted out loud that they'd thought the play, with all its elves and talking flowers and dum-di-dum-happy-ever-after ending was awful.

"Yeah. It would have been cool," said Flash. "Maybe you should be a poet instead of a chef."

"No way," said Eclaire "I'm gonna open Fatso's restaurant... but maybe I could do poems on the menu?"

"Yeah and have Owl singing them in the bar," said Lizzy.

"By the way, Dolores Azores gave me these for saving the show,"

interrupted Owl, reaching into an old carrier bag and pulling out a nearly new, incredibly smart pair of silver sprayed trainers. "She wore them in the show, but she says they're too small and that's why she tripped. B-but of course they're m-much too big for me. I wonder if they'll fit any of you?" she said this as casually as possible, knowing that Flash was desperate for a pair.

Flash's eyes lit up like beacons but she was much too proud to say anything. Eclaire and Lizzy dutifully tried them on and pretended they didn't fit. They pushed and shoved and squeaked and groaned and didn't fool anybody. Owl was reminded of the Ugly Sisters in Cinderella. "You try them Flash," she said.

"Oh, all right," Flash shrugged.

They were a perfect fit.

"I suppose I might as well have them if no one else wants them," muttered Flash.

"D'you know?" said Owl "The b-best thing about all this is my family being so pleased. See..." she gulped. "They're getting me drama lessons and all. I m-mean they would have died laughing a few days ago if I'd mentioned acting. And there's one other thing..."

"What's that Owl?" asked Lizzy.

"Well I d-don't really like to say... b-but when little B-Brian didn't turn up, I had a horrible idea you might have all, you know, k-kidnapped him, or drowned him or something like that... It was such a relief to know you hadn't... In fact, he made a point of saying how incredibly kind you all were to him..."

Eclaire blushed. She felt a bit queasy about having given Brian two more whole bags of her special delicious nuclear nougat just before the show began. But she didn't think it could have affected him really, even though she'd left another two bags for him to have in the interval. She had secretly hoped it might make him queasy, but she hadn't wanted him to be quite so sick. Better not to mention it.

Lizzy blushed too, she glanced nervously at Eclaire and was relieved to see she wasn't going to own up. She now felt that maybe she shouldn't have horsed around a bit with Brian before the show. At least, not after giving him all those sweets... all she'd done was whirl him round and round by his ankles incredibly fast. He'd loved it of course, and asked for more, so naturally she had obliged and done it again. And again. But she did wonder if it might have made him feel a little unsteady... Better not to mention it.

But it was Flash who felt the worst of all. She didn't feel too bad about Brian, because the others had both stuffed him with sweeties too, but she felt she had done something really bad, looking back. Realising (wrongly, as it turned out) that they'd failed to make Brian sick, she had slipped backstage in the interval and put a conker inside one of Dolores Azores's ice maiden's silver sprayed trainers. She'd hoped it might just trip her up, and luckily that's all it had done. But supposing it had been worse?

Supposing she had fallen down a whole flight of stairs and broken her neck? Flash went icy at the thought. She felt particularly bad now she had Dolores's very same pair of trainers. 'I'll just have to give them away,' she vowed sorrowfully to herself. Maybe she should tell the others?

But no, Dolores was fine. Better not to mention it. And she CERTAINLY wasn't going to mention the two vast ice creams she had bought for Brian during the interval.

No way.